WITHERING WOODS

ANGELA CORBETT

Midnight
Sands
Publishing

WITHERING WOODS

ANGELA CORBETT

Published in the United States of America by Midnight Sands Publishing

PROLOGUE

*B*ethany Cross's legs burned as she raced through the trees, feet faltering on the uneven earth and rocks. She wasn't as fast as she used to be, and she regretted venturing out here alone. Breaking the rules of Withering Woods had been a mistake...one that would come at a high cost if she didn't get to safety soon. The trees gave her some cover, but she could practically hear the whooshing noise stalking her from above—the leaves like the blades of a helicopter interspersed with agonizing screams. There was one spot in the forest she could take refuge...if she could get there. She looked over her shoulder as she ran, her heart pounding from the exertion. She'd spent decades doing research and investigating. She knew the warnings—knew she shouldn't be here past nightfall. But she was so close to being finished with her film.

Stories.

Myths.

Urban legends.

That's what the skeptics had always said the rumors were —and what she'd never believed. There are those who embrace the unexplained. And those who don't. Both groups are at great risk, but for different reasons: the people who know what exists on the fringe can't stop hunting it, and the people who don't believe become easy targets.

Starlight filtered through the sparse leaves as Bethany came to an area that was far more open to the sky. The lack of cover meant she'd lost her ability to hide. The noises above her grew louder, taking her attention away from the ground she was trying to navigate. Her foot hit a divot in the path and her ankle rolled. She collapsed hard, tumbling down an embankment until she came to rest against a tree. She took a deep breath, wincing as she tried to rotate her foot. Getting to safety would be harder now. She froze, listening and no longer hearing or seeing her winged stalkers. She closed her eyes and said a silent thank you for the reprieve. With the reassurance that she was still alive, she spent a minute taking stock of her equipment. The camera was destroyed, pieces of it scattered along behind her, a trail of metal and plastic leading to her current spot against the tree. She sighed. It wouldn't be cheap to replace, but hopefully her footage would still be salvageable. She leaned over to pick up the pieces, and that's when she noticed the glass.

"No, no, no, no, no," she said, her whisper getting louder and more urgent with each word. The jagged, multicolored pieces were strewn even more haphazardly than her camera, but unlike her camera, the glass was invaluable—it could keep her alive if she was attacked. Her heart sank at the realization and she made an immediate decision: she would run. It was her only hope. She stood, pain shooting all the way from the tips of her toes up through her leg. Broken bones could be fixed, but nothing could be done if she lost her life in the woods. She took a tentative step, then another. Limping along and trying to make as little noise as possible. It wasn't enough.

Bethany only made it a few feet when she heard the whooshing noise and the ringing peal before they descended. Her eyes were wide with terror as she tried to pinpoint exactly where the sound originated. But there were several piercing screams blending together to create a demonic melody. She tried to flee the nightmare she was entangled in. But even on two good ankles, she wouldn't have been able to escape them.

She felt the first slash across her chest, then another on her arm. The lashes continued like fiery whips across her skin. She tried to fight back for a time, but without the glass, she had no hope of escaping. Eventually she retreated to a place in her head where she couldn't feel pain. Absently, she wondered if authorities would even be able to identify her body when this was over. She should have taken more precautions...called on more protection. She should have stayed home and avoided the woods and its legends entirely.

"Should" was such a pointless word.

A winged shadow, blacker than night, hovered over her, its bright eyes the only feature she could make out on its face. She felt her life force starting to drain as darkness seeped into her like it was flowing through her veins. It was the end; she knew it. She had so many things she'd wanted to do and now she wouldn't get the chance. She wished she'd spent more time with her son, Ledger. She didn't want him to worry, and she definitely didn't want him to come looking for her. But she knew he would. He was stubborn like that. She smiled at the thought, grateful her final memories wouldn't be of the monster stealing her life.

She turned her head away from the shadow above her and as she did, another figure came into her line of vision moving with animal-like precision, too quickly for her eyes to track. Abruptly, the grim shadow above her was gone and a familiar face replaced the torture. Bethany looked at her

3

friend through blurry vision. Her rescuer was wearing black clothes, complete with a cloak and hood. The hooded figure pressed lightly against Bethany's wounds, checking her vitals.

Bethany heard her friend's rattled sigh.

"Is...it...bad?" Bethany asked, already knowing the answer.

The figure sliced her head down once. "I'm sorry," the kind voice said. "I didn't get here in time. I tried to stop them."

Bethany couldn't feel the pain, and was aware the numbness wasn't a good sign. "I...know. Thank...you." Her vision started to distort—flashes of light like starbursts forming in front of her, a kaleidoscope of galaxies stretching in all directions for her to explore. She smiled, and thought of her Ledger. How much he'd like to explore these new worlds. One day he would. And she'd be there to explore with him when it was time. But not yet.

The *not yet* thought kept her tethered to her body. She knew Ledger would search for her. He was driven by the same need for answers that she'd always been consumed by. And when the police couldn't explain her death—and she knew they wouldn't be able to—he'd try to figure it out on his own. She couldn't let the same thing happen to him.

With her last bit of energy, Bethany mumbled, "Ledger. Watch out for him." Her eyes were wide with anxiousness, needing this last reassurance from her young friend before she'd allow herself to ascend, and the pain to leave her.

Her friend nodded and put a warm hand over Bethany's. The shattered glass on the ground reflected the stunning starlight above, and the hooded figure watched through tear-filled eyes as Bethany's soul returned to the sky.

CHAPTER 1

*W*elcome to Withering Woods where we're known for our picturesque archway of blooming red roses! While you're here, be sure not to miss the majestic one-hundred-foot waterfall that ends in a beautiful blue pond so clear you can see the glass-like rocks on the bottom. Hike to Longfellow's Peak for a breathtaking view of the valley below, and then take the zipline back down through a mass of statuesque trees. See the petrified rock formations, and rappel past ancient petroglyphs. You'll be left with memories to last a lifetime! Please note, however, that our forest closes at twilight. On your way out, you might notice the arch of blood red roses starting to wither—a sign you've left just in time. Withering Woods is not responsible for what happens if you decide to linger beyond the roses past curfew. Should you choose to stay, be advised that there are three rules you must follow in Withering Woods after dark.

1. Do not look up.
2. Do not look behind you.
3. And if you hear the screams... Run.

. . .

Ledger hit play again and listened to the voiceover as he watched the introduction fade from a serene, peaceful scene, to one that could invoke the most spine-chilling of nightmares.

He'd memorized the script, a result of listening to it repeatedly for the past two years. He'd grown up hearing his mom tell this, and other similar stories. She'd been a documentary filmmaker who had devoted her career to exploring fantasy, folklore, and stories of the unexplained. This was one of her best pieces. Unfortunately, he didn't have the ending. It had been destroyed with her camera in Withering Woods two years ago...the night she'd died.

He'd joined her on some of her adventures when he was younger; helping her research stories, look for clues, and make movies. The memories were lifelines for him now. The grief had been unbearable at first and he'd become a shell of his former self. With time, it had improved, but the empty space in his heart was a constant reminder she was gone. He'd never hear her voice again, or laugh with her while they watched silly movies, or take a road trip to investigate the newest story of the unexplained. His mom's adventures were over, and that was one of the hardest realizations to accept.

It would have been easier to move on if he had answers. But he didn't. Investigators hadn't been able to figure out exactly what happened to her. The case had been closed months ago, against his wishes. He'd used his grief as fuel to try and get the answers he desperately needed for closure. The police, while kind, had told him in no uncertain terms that the case had been solved. It was a heart attack. Plain and simple. The deep scratches on her arms and chest a result of her fall down the side of the hill. He didn't buy it. His mom had no history of heart disease in her family. She never missed a yearly checkup and she'd just had her annual physical a month before her death. She was fine, and there was no reason her heart should have given out.

The psychologist he was referred to, and the police department, dismissed his claims of foul play blaming his suspicions instead on a grieving heart. The word "delusional" had been bandied about. If she'd died under normal circumstances, he might have been willing to accept the heart attack answer. If she hadn't been found in a collage of broken glass and equipment—equipment she valued almost as much as the relationships she held closest—and if her neck and arms hadn't been ripped, scratches so fierce and deep they looked like they'd been made by claws, he might have been able to close the case in his mind as well. But he'd spent his life trying to make sense of the unexplained and there were too many circumstances around her death that made no sense. If the police wouldn't try to figure it out, Ledger would.

Ledger knew the rules of Withering Woods, and every time he visited, he did so intending to break them. He passed by the fabled rose bush archway at the entrance to the woods. The rose petals that hadn't yet fallen to the ground were wrinkled and colored with a deathly grey hue. The vibrant flowers were gorgeous during the day, but withered every night, only to have other buds replace them like clockwork the next morning. Despite many attempts to figure out the rose life-cycle mystery, no one knew why the roses died after sunset. It was another thing that made the stories about the woods seem plausible.

Withering Woods was legendary for its strange occurrences and supernatural sightings. People claimed to have seen everything from vampires to the Mothman roaming the landscape. But the most notorious story by far was the

Screamers of Withering Woods. No one had ever caught them on film, but accounts were always similar: wraithlike, winged flying figures that hunted from above before swooping down to attack. They were faceless except for glowing eyes of various colors. They hunted by scent, and when they found their prey, they would start a chorus of demonic screams before descending to steal the life from their victims.

Ledger wasn't a stranger to the paranormal—he'd seen too much to disbelieve. But no one had ever been able to offer evidence of the existence of the Screamers...at least, not that he knew of. It's why his mom had been out here when she died; she'd been looking for the proof. His gut told him she'd found it, or found something even worse. Urban legends usually sprang from a grain of truth, and sometimes those legends turned out to have more reality to them than anyone could imagine. His mom had made it her life's work to investigate stories like the Screamers of Withering Woods, and try to find the evidence that fueled them.

He surveyed the woods as he looked down the embankment—a spot he'd grieved at and investigated for the past two years. The crime scene photos were etched into his mind like an initial carved into a tree. They were a part of him now, always there in the background of his thoughts; a morbid reminder of his loss, and a visual that he'd never be able to forget or unsee.

Police said she'd likely fallen down this embankment after she'd had the heart attack. She was found at the bottom, her equipment in pieces and glass scattered around her. They had no explanation for the glass, but found some shards in her bag as well and speculated that she'd been carrying it...a bottle of some sort.

He reached in his pocket, his fingers going over a piece of the smooth, colored glass like a worry stone. He'd been out here many times, retracing her steps. It didn't matter that the seasons had come and gone, and clues that might have once been here had washed away. He wasn't looking for the answers on the surface, the ones that could be easily found. He was looking for the answers that needed to be excavated. One way or another, he'd figure out what had killed his mom. It was just a matter of time and persistence.

Ledger bent down, examining the soil. The sun was beginning to set and light through the trees hit the ground in a beautiful pattern of chaos. He followed the light, his gaze landing on an area in front of him that he'd never noticed during previous visits. At first glance, it simply looked like several shrubs that had grown together, but as he focused on the foliage, he noticed the shrubs seemed to be concealing something. He pushed up from his crouch and walked over to the area, shoving aside branches and leaves. A corridor extended beyond the foliage...a tunnel of sorts. He pulled out his flashlight and started to make his way through the path. It was shaped like an arch, and maybe six feet tall...shorter than he was. He ducked to protect his head while trying to stay vigilant. An earthy, wet smell hit his nostrils and his feet sunk down, the ground soft from lack of sunlight. He walked about twenty feet before the tunnel opened up into a large, square shaped clearing, surrounded by tall stone on each side. Trees grew out of cracks in the rock, their branches looming like a canopy.

As he looked around—in front, to the sides, and behind him—a foreboding feeling washed over him. It wasn't a feeling he was unaccustomed to. From a young age, he'd learned that he needed to trust his instincts above all else; that his subconscious was far more aware than he was. The hair on the back of his neck stood up and he heard a high-pitched wail. His eyes immediately darted up to the trees, looking for the source of the sound as he held his flashlight.

The light was heavy enough that it could also be used as a weapon—provided the attacker was something tangible. He didn't have to wait long to find out. Darkness settled over the cavern like the sun had blinked out of existence, switched off as easily as a light switch. And in the darkness, a shadow, black as pitch, came toward him with the grace and size of a panther. But panthers didn't live in Withering Woods, and they didn't have wings, or glowing eyes. His mind immediately tried to make sense of it, and failed. Making sense of it was wasted effort. He needed action. But he didn't know how to fight this threat. He tried to back away from it and stumbled, catching himself as he fell. The screams continued as it drew closer and he found it difficult to draw a complete breath.

He put his hand in the air, trying to stop the shadow and speak the spell of protection his mom had taught him long ago. But it was too late for even that. He had the sudden realization that he was going to die, possibly in the same way as his mom, without the answers he'd needed to put him—and her—at peace.

Darkness and despair seemed to be seeping into his body. He wanted to fight, but his energy felt completely depleted. He swiped at the shadow with his flashlight. It made a shrieking noise, and then without warning, the screaming became louder. His eyes darted up and he saw another figure —human shaped—fly through the air, battling the shadow. The human figure moved like the wind, so fast he could hardly track it.

"Watch out for the animal!" he yelled, for lack of a better description of the shadow.

He heard the figure murmuring something and before he knew it, the shadow was gone. He had no idea where it had disappeared to, but the darkness that had seemed to take root in his soul slowly dissipated.

Twilight returned to the cavern—the stones, trees, and tunnel he'd entered through once again visible. The figure that had shown up out of nowhere and fought the shadow was there too—leaning against the rock, blending into the stone with the ability of a chameleon. He studied it. Black leather pants. A black shirt. Hooded black cloak. Like a human version of the grim reaper. Nothing about the figure seemed welcoming, and he wondered what its motivations were...and which was more dangerous: the shadow that had been chased away, or the figure standing before him.

"Not an animal," came a lyrical, feminine voice.

His eyes widened. He wasn't sure what shocked him more: the fact that he'd just been attacked by something he didn't believe to be human, or the fact that the person who'd defended him was half his size and female. "You're a woman?"

He couldn't see it, but he could feel her glare fifteen feet away. "You broke the Withering Woods rules," she said instead of answering his obvious question. "You're an idiot, and you shouldn't be here." Her voice was hot liquid being poured over ice and every nerve ending in his body felt like it was tied to a string and being pulled directly toward her. He tried to shake off the feeling, but couldn't. It was like he knew her in some visceral, unexplainable way. She'd saved him from what he believed was probably a Screamer, and she obviously knew more about the woods than he did. He was intrigued, mystified, and wanted to unwrap all of her secrets —yet she'd hardly spoken to him. He hadn't even seen her face.

He stood, brushing dirt off his jeans. He cursed under his breath at how ridiculous he'd probably looked, and that he'd needed saving at all. He'd been trained and knew how to protect himself, physically, mentally, and emotionally. He just hadn't done it well. It was a good thing she'd been there to help him; though his lack of self-reliance and his need to depend on another had wounded his pride. But he always gave credit where credit was due, and this woman was the reason he was alive. "I'd take offense to that if it wasn't coming from someone who sounds like she knows what she's talking about." And had the voice of a dark angel, but he was already embarrassed enough and didn't need to add that bit of information as well.

She stared at this naïve human, her gaze going over his jeans and ridiculous bright yellow shirt. If he'd been standing in the middle of the woods with a spotlight on his location, it would have drawn less attention than his shirt color choice. Her eyes pierced him, looking for signs of weakness. She knew his type: the kind who wanted an adventure but didn't think about consequences. She'd saved her fair share of them over the years—and had failed others, a fact she'd never forgive herself for. "You're out here at night. Alone. You shouldn't be," she reiterated. "Not only that, but you looked up, you looked behind you, you heard the screams, and you didn't run."

His lips tipped up in a charming smile. "Want to know a secret?"

She didn't answer.

He went on anyway, "It's not the first time I've broken the rules of Withering Woods."

Her breathing changed to shorter inhales, her annoyance evident. "Then you clearly have a death wish."

He took a moment to consider the statement that seemed like more of a warning before he asked, "What's your name?"

She crossed her arms over her chest. "Why does that matter?"

"Social etiquette," he said, lifting his shoulder. "Common courtesy. And so I can thank you."

She didn't answer.

He studied her more. She was still standing in the exact same spot, her legs shoulder width apart. She seemed abnormally aware of everything around her, like she'd done this before. The waves of distaste rolling off of her let him know she wasn't the least bit interested in becoming friends. It didn't dissuade him in the slightest. Aside from the fact that he wanted to know more about her, he realized if she knew the area, she might be able to help him find more clues about the death of his mom. She wasn't someone he wanted to piss off, and she also wasn't someone he wanted to lose contact with. Luckily he had a thick skin, and he wasn't easily discouraged. The corner of his lips ticked up in an amused smile. "Wow, you really don't like me. Good thing I'm persistent." He walked toward her and put his hand out. Her hood left most of her facial features in shadow, but he was able to make out one of her eyes beneath the cloak. It was a brilliant shade of turquoise. "I'm Ledger Cross."

Her whole body stiffened at his words, her hand holding steady at her side. "Ledger Cross," she said slowly.

He gave her a look. "I know, it sounds like a superhero name or something but don't worry, I'm not one."

"I'd feel better if you were," she mumbled, barely loud enough for him to hear. At least then he'd have some sort of defense. At the moment, she was it. And now that she knew his name, she also knew something else about him: that this idiot was determined to keep coming to the woods, breaking the rules, and putting himself in harm's way. She needed to stop that from happening.

This was the man she'd promised to keep out of the forest. Away from the threats. Away from the same things that had killed his mom—someone she thought of as a friend...her only one.

The little bit of daylight that remained was slowly

13

winking out. She'd planned to work tonight, but she needed to deal with her guest first.

She walked toward the tunnel, past him, her floral scent hitting him like he was suddenly sitting in the midst of a rose garden. He watched her start through the opening, then stop. She turned her head to the side so he could hear her say, "Come with me."

He probably should have questioned her command more, but he was too curious about the mysterious woman who seemed to view him as nothing more than an annoyance. He wanted the chance to ask her about his mom, and he wasn't going to give up that opportunity.

They came out of the tunnel and he followed her silently down a path he'd never seen. It was a trail, but looked like someone had taken pains to try and hide that fact. After about ten minutes of walking, they came to a house in the middle of the woods. The house was red brick, two windows on the front bookending a door that was painted cobalt blue. It was two stories tall and old, but well maintained. Ivy climbed the walls, a pretty strangulation of the mortar. The thing that shocked him the most though wasn't the out of place, quaint home isolated in the woods. It was the vibrant roses in shades of pink, red, and white that surrounded the home. Roses didn't stay alive in Withering Woods after dark...at least not in any part of the woods he'd ever explored.

"There are roses here," he said, his tone carrying his disbelief. "And they're alive after dark. In Withering Woods."

She nodded. "It's the only place they live."

"How is that possible?"

"Because they're protected here."

He wanted to ask her more about that but she pushed through the door, hanging her bag on a hook beside it and continuing into the next room.

Ledger paused at the threshold, tentative as he looked inside. "You live here?"

She turned back to him. "No, I just walk into random, unlocked houses in the woods and make myself at home."

His lips slid into a grin, interest sparking in his eyes.

She frowned. Her sarcasm—which on the rare times she'd had contact with other humans had usually been a solid defense mechanism to get them to stop asking questions and leave her alone—didn't seem to be working on Ledger. She liked her quiet life. Alone. In her house. Without people. It hadn't been easy at first, but she'd lived in solitude for so long now that she'd learned how to be on her own. She needed no one, and she wanted to be clear about that fact.

He stepped inside the entryway that opened into a larger living area. His eyes moved about the room, searching for the familiar to grasp onto, as well as clues about her and who she was, but he was having a hard time adjusting to the darkness. "You don't have electricity?" he asked.

She changed location in the room almost silently; the only sound alerting him to movement was the rustle of the cloak against her legs. "Electricity is spotty."

"You're out here alone," he said.

It was part statement, part question, and one she purposely didn't answer. She watched him as he took in the room, making assumptions and judgments about her with his discoveries. She didn't fault him for being curious and thorough—couldn't really—since she was doing something similar at the same time: assessing him and his motives.

His eyes flickered and she could feel his gaze on her in the darkness like he was trying to hold her paralyzed with his attention. That trick didn't work on her; she wasn't so easily consumed. She struck a match, the flame flashing in front of her and growing brighter as she lit a candle. "There are a lot of things in the woods that can hurt you," she said, deliberately not answering his earlier question. "Especially at night."

"I know," he answered. He paused and then asked, "Are you one of them?"

Her eyes went over him, her perusal taking him in inch by inch. He was a giant who had almost gotten himself killed and then invaded her space because she couldn't let him wander the woods alone and she needed him in a safe place. Bethany had told her about Ledger, but had failed to mention his litany of attributes. Though she was reluctant to admit it, he certainly wasn't hard to look at. He had to be at least six-foot-three. His hair was golden and his eyes were the lightest shade of green she'd ever seen—so pale it almost looked like he had no irises at all. Her experience with men was limited, but she knew from the moment she saw him that this particular one would be trouble. She ran her tongue slowly over her lips. "Not today."

A shiver ran through him. And it wasn't from fear. There was a general uneasiness brought on by his earlier experience in the woods...and an attraction to this enigmatic woman that he wasn't completely comfortable with, but the feeling was one he didn't want to dismiss either. With effort, he pulled his attention away from her, taking in more of the house. It was clean, the furniture modern—a contrast to the historic exterior of the home. The living room extended down a wide hall into what he assumed was a kitchen. Withering Woods had cabins, but he'd never seen an actual home. He had no idea how she'd managed to buy a house in the middle of a national forest, but given the age of the structure, he assumed it was likely grandfathered in through an inheritance of some sort.

She leaned against the wall, halfway in the room, halfway out. "You should stay here tonight."

His eyes must have shown his surprise at the suggestion because she gave a soft laugh at his expression.

"I'm not saying you have to," she said. "I'm just saying it would be safer."

He gave a derisive snort. "Here? You think I'm safer here with a girl who won't even take her hood off so I can see her face, and refuses to tell me her name?"

Her one visibile turquoise eye flashed behind the hood. "Nothing in the woods will bother someone under my roof, and my protection."

The word "nothing" hadn't escaped his notice. And neither had the implication that he was somehow being protected by her. "What does that mean?"

She leaned down, her voice a whisper against his neck. "It means you should say thank you."

She started to walk out of the room. "The couch pulls out into a bed. If you need something to do, there are books in the library down the hall. The bathroom is next to the library. If you do touch the books, put them back where you found them."

He watched her walk away from him, equal parts perplexed and intrigued. After less than a minute, she was back, handing him sheets and a pillow, her hood still covering her face. "Thanks," he said, standing to pull the couch out and make his bed.

She nodded once and then started toward the door.

"Where are you going?" he asked.

"To work. I'll be back in the morning."

"You're just going to trust a stranger to stay in your house all night?"

She stopped and inclined her head in his direction. "Are you planning to do something you shouldn't?"

"No."

"Then you'll be safe here. I'll see you in the morning."

She started out the door and then paused, one hand on the door frame. She turned her head and over her shoulder said, "Jolie."

His brow wrinkled in confusion. "I beg your pardon?"

"You asked my name. It's Jolie. And you're going to want to keep this locked."

She walked out, the door clicking shut behind her.

CHAPTER 2

*J*olie's warning to keep the door locked had given Ledger pause. Was she saying that he should lock her out? Or lock out all the other things stalking around in the woods? What did she do for work? Did she have a regular job? Or did her "work" encompass the same thing she'd been doing earlier—fighting beings that most people didn't even believe in? He had a feeling the answer was closer to his second speculation than his first. The investigator in him had wanted to run out and follow her, his camera in hand, getting proof of whatever she was encountering—it's what his mom would have done. He considered it for a while, but then an overwhelming desire to sleep had overtaken him. He'd been so tired. The ongoing search for answers about his mom's death, coupled with the unending grief had taken its toll and he'd slept through the night like he'd been drugged.

He woke early in the morning, the door still locked like he'd left it. He moved quietly about the house in case Jolie had come home and was asleep. As he walked around her home, he tried to get a better idea of the woman who'd saved his life. Her living space was comfortable, clean, and minimal. As he wandered, he realized he was still alone and she hadn't returned yet. He padded into the kitchen filled with retro appliances, a butcher block countertop, and a modern subway tile backsplash. He saw a notepad on the countertop and wrote down his name and phone number. He didn't know when she'd be back, and he wanted to talk to her more about what had happened the night before.

He put the note next to the coffee maker, and immediately felt the pangs of hunger in his stomach. He hadn't eaten for at least sixteen hours. Coffee and breakfast sounded good, but he didn't want to use her food and be any more of an imposition than he already had been. After opening some cabinets and drawers, he found a cup and opted for a glass of water instead of coffee. He took it with him to the library. He thought he could read for an hour or so and see if she returned; if not, he'd leave and come back later. He didn't want to be a burden, and staying here unchaperoned felt like the ultimate intrusion on her space.

She'd mentioned the library last night but this was his first look at it—and it was breathtaking. Tall, mahogany shelves lined the walls, full of books of every kind, both old and new. Fiction, non-fiction, and even text books. Jolie's tastes were wide-ranging. He perused the shelves, and when he got to the section on the paranormal, he wished he could take a few home to read himself. There were newer releases too, some he recognized. One series was pulled out, and it looked like a book was missing. He glanced around the room and found it on the table next to a creamy white chaise lounge. He smiled as he picked the tome up. He knew the book, and the series; maybe that could be some common ground for them to talk and get to know each other better. As he scanned the book summary, he realized the book she was currently reading wasn't the newest in the series. He furrowed his brow and checked the shelf—she didn't have the newest, and final, book. The series ending title had released a month ago. He'd already read it twice, and was surprised she didn't have it yet.

He put the book back on the table next to the chaise and as he did, light glinted off of something, catching his eye. Several pieces of beautifully colored glass sat on the windowsill in various shapes. Some were molded into dainty flowers with delicate petals, others looked like abstract shapes with colors weaving through the glass. Their beauty alone would have made him stop and take notice, but it wasn't just the artisanship. The color variations in the glass were exceptionally familiar.

He went to the living room and grabbed his coat. Reaching inside the pocket, he pulled out the smooth piece of glass that he carried with him wherever he went. He walked back to the library and held his piece next to the abstract glass sitting on the windowsill. It looked identical. Ledger pursed his lips, a thousand thoughts running though his head. Jolie had glass pieces incredibly similar to the shards that had been found shattered around his mom. That couldn't be a coincidence. Did Jolie have something to do with his mom's death? His stomach churned at the thought. No longer caring about privacy, he immediately moved through the rest of the house, looking for more signs of the glass.

He found them in a room upstairs. It was heavily secured, and not by locks. Jolie's knowledge of wards and spells almost surpassed his own.

Emotion warred in his chest. The thought of the woman who had captivated him from the moment she swooped down, dark and graceful to battle the shadow trying to attack him, being involved in his mom's death, made bile rise in his throat. He needed to think and get a handle on his emotions, but he couldn't do it here, surrounded by more questions than answers.

He slipped his glass piece back into his pocket, put the books back where he'd found them, and placed his used cup in the dishwasher. He grabbed his things and made sure the door was locked behind him before he left...like a ghost who had never been there at all.

Ledger was fast asleep before Jolie had finally ventured out into the woods the night before. She'd considered staying home. She didn't like the idea of a stranger in her house, rummaging through her things. But he was Bethany's son, so he wasn't a stranger entirely. She'd uttered a simple sleep spell after she'd walked out the door, and made sure he'd been breathing deeply, his eyes fluttering under their lids before she'd finally left for her nightly patrol. She knew the spell would keep him asleep until morning.

The night had been typical of all her nights; stalking the woods, searching for the things that might cause others harm. Withering Woods had urban legends about everything from fairies to ghosts, and she'd run into her fair share of fantastical beings. But the ones she was looking for specifically were the sinister Screamers—wraithlike, winged figures of magical origin who derived their power from taking the life force of those they attacked. The longer and more drawn out the death was, the more power they took. And Withering Woods had a lot of them. Shadowy and see-through, they could easily change their shape and blend in with their surroundings. Their ability to fly made it easy for them to spot prey—people usually look for threats at eye-level, most don't look up, and if they do, they wish they hadn't.

Thanks to the tutelage of the woman who'd raised her—

Sola a powerful priestess of magic—Jolie knew how to capture the Screamers. Spelled, specially made glass orbs drew the Screamers in, hypnotizing them with the colors and sounds emanating from the orbs. Once inside the glass prisons, the Screamers couldn't be released...unless the orb was shattered.

After Sola's death, Jolie had decided that finding and ridding the world of the Screamers was her life's purpose. The Screamers were evil, soulless, and selfish. They didn't care who they killed: child or adult, and only wanted the power that came from death.

She knew, because her parents had died saving her from one.

Jolie was still looking for the Screamer who had taken the people she loved most from her, and clawed its mark across the right side of her face and down her neck leaving deep, jagged scars on her body. The Screamer had stolen whatever normal future she might have had and insured she would forever be viewed with odd, pitying stares from anyone who set eyes on her. She remembered going into town with Sola as a child and the look of kindness people gave her when they saw the unblemished left side of her face, followed immediately by abject horror when their eyes fell on the right, taking in her scars. Those expressions were seared into her memory.

Her differences had made her feel ashamed of her appearance. The pointing and laughter from other children had hurt more than any injury she'd ever had. The need to be accepted was an ache at the bottom of a hole in her soul that she knew would never be filled. For a long time, it had held her paralyzed. But Sola had taught Jolie that the only person Jolie could change or control was herself. When Jolie pushed the emotions out of the way and thought logically about that, she was able to accept Sola's advice and move forward building her life—one she knew she would never share with another. Pity was worse than any pain she'd suffered and she'd vowed to live her life in isolation in the woods. But she would continue fighting the Screamers to keep as many people as possible from having to experience what she already had.

When she got back this morning, Ledger was already gone. He'd left a note next to the coffee maker thanking her, and left his phone number as well, asking her to call him. She folded the note and put it away for safe keeping, knowing full well it was a number that she'd never use. An unexpected sadness washed over her. She took a minute to analyze her feelings. What had she been expecting? A friend? Something more? Both were ridiculous, and not at all what she needed—or wanted, she added, trying to convince herself. She had a goal and she needed to focus on that, not a schoolgirl crush. If Ledger was anything like his mom though, he would be back. She needed to nip this in the bud and stop him from coming back to Withering Woods. He was going to get himself killed and she didn't need another life on her conscience.

She went upstairs to her office and slowly retrieved three brightly colored glass orbs from her pack: one purple, one green, one blue. She gently placed them on stands on a shelf, then closed and secured the shelf. The orbs were dangerous and needed more than a simple lock, which was why she uttered a binding spell as she placed them.

She moved down the hall to the bathroom and showered, then fell asleep, the previous day and night catching up to her. When she woke, she wandered downstairs and started the coffee maker, then put a piece of bread in her toaster. Despite using candles the night before with Ledger—which she'd done deliberately so he'd be less likely to see her face and her scars—her home had all the modern amenities. Fresh water came from a well, the house had a septic tank, and her electricity was harnessed by solar power. She had the internet, television, and most importantly, Netflix.

She took her coffee mug with her and moved to her favorite room in the house: the library. She picked up the well-worn book she'd been reading from her side table. She was currently re-reading one of her favorite series before diving into the final book that had recently been released. She loved stories. They were places she could escape to and ways for her to live her dreams—dreams she knew she'd never be able to experience on her own, in the woods, a prison she'd created out of self-preservation.

The library was the largest room in the house. A massive assortment of books lined shelves that were built from floor to ceiling. Sola had started the collection as a young child and had continued growing it her whole life. It was a tradition Jolie was happy to carry on. Her phone was with her at all times, and she constantly searched for new books to add to her hardcover library, and to put on her eReader. Ebooks made it so much easier to be an introvert.

Her favorite thing to do was to sit in her library, the musky smell of pages and ink permeating her senses as she spread out on the chaise lounge next to the fireplace and got lost in the paragraphs of a world she'd never experience in reality—one of friends, family, parties, dating, and love. She could live them from her library though, where she was safe and didn't have to hide herself or feel ashamed of what she looked like.

As she read a particularly romantic scene, her thoughts drifted unwillingly to Ledger. She stopped, pulled from the story as she realized just who she'd been envisioning as the hero to her heroine. She took a moment to examine her feelings. She'd just met him. She knew nothing about him other than the things Bethany had said during their few meetings.

She'd had no idea he was so tall, or that his jawline was so defined. Bethany hadn't mentioned he exuded masculinity on a colossal scale. And when she'd saved him, the look in his eyes hadn't been anger or a punch to his ego—like some of the other men she'd helped in similar circumstances—instead, she'd seen respect. The feeling had made her heart beat faster and though she'd never experienced it personally before, she'd read enough romance novels to know she'd been attracted to him. It was a vexing realization, and one she didn't know what to do with. Jolie hoped it was a passing emotion, and not something that would continue, especially because she was hopeful that for the sake of his safety, she would never see Ledger Cross again.

The thought saddened her. For all of her avoidance of people, she'd liked having him here. A surprising emptiness had settled in her chest when she'd come home and found him already gone. But no amount of unhappiness and regret would make him even the least bit interested in her and her flaws. She needed to move forward. Alone. Like she always had.

Jolie spent the rest of the day reading.

When night fell, she did what she always did. She hunted.

CHAPTER 3

*T*he night had been long and unproductive. She'd been distracted by thoughts of Ledger—of the yearning for a normal life he'd stirred inside of her, and the sorrow she felt knowing normal was not her path. She needed to get a handle on her emotions because even though she'd warned him away, she was certain he'd be back. He was Bethany's son, after all, and she knew he was as tenacious as Bethany had been. Jolie had no doubt Ledger's presence in Withering Woods meant he was looking for clues about his mother and her death. Jolie had answers. The question was whether or not he could handle it if she shared them. She checked herself. She tried not to make choices based on what she believed another person's reaction would be. She should give him the information and let him accept it, or not. It wasn't her problem. And maybe if she gave him the details, he'd stop coming out to the woods and risk suffering the same fate as his mom.

When she returned home, she'd taken a quick shower before collapsing into bed. She woke to a heavy knock on the door. After the initial shock, Jolie narrowed her eyes. She never had visitors. Ever. She quickly checked the mirror, making sure the deep part of her long, dark brown hair was in place, a silky security blanket covering the right side of her face.

She grabbed a stun gun from her drawer and walked to the door. She let her hand rest on the knob for a few seconds while she listened; she didn't hear anything strange. She turned the knob and pulled open the door, stifling a gasp. Ledger stood on her porch, his sandy hair swept in different directions like it had been combed by the wind. The front of a sage colored t-shirt was tucked into dark jeans, held up by a distressed black belt buckle. Ropey muscles in his thick forearms were highlighted by the strain of holding the two bags he had in his hands.

She inhaled a rattled breath, the romantic, unrealistic side of her warring with the sensible one. The truth was that she wanted Ledger here. Despite her aloofness, she wanted a man to want to get to know her. She wanted someone to see her for who she was, instead of only seeing scars and making presumptions. Those thoughts aside, she also knew the woods were dangerous and Ledger shouldn't be making visits a habit. She yearned for a friend—and more—but not at the expense of a life. Even if she could keep him safe... teach him the things she'd taught Bethany and be there to fight with him so he wouldn't suffer the same fate as others who'd disregarded the warnings and remained in the woods after darkness. And even if he did want to get to know her better, the reality was that he wouldn't want any of those things after he knew about her past and saw her scars.

She looked up at the sky. Still afternoon, but it would be dark in a few hours and the woods would be unsafe for someone without the proper knowledge and skills. Ledger's mom had had them both, and even that couldn't save her.

Jolie narrowed her eyes, one of them still shrouded by her hair. "What are you doing here?"

Ledger was having a hard time maintaining his composure. He hadn't seen her face before and even now, it was partly covered by silky hair that his fingers ached to touch. She was absolutely gorgeous. Her cheekbones were high, framing her beautiful, captivating turquoise eyes—the one he could see at least. Her nose came to a perfectly rounded tip, and her lips were shaped like a heart, full and asking to be kissed. He shook himself out of his trance and answered, "I was in the neighborhood and decided to stop by."

She pressed her lips together before saying, "You can't keep doing this."

He arched a brow. "Can't keep doing what?"

"Coming out here," she said, leaning against the door frame. "You need to stay out of Withering Woods. For your own good."

He walked over to the edge of the porch, looking beyond the house, then around at the trees before coming back to stand in front of her. "Is there something I should be afraid of?" he said, asking the same question he'd asked the night they met.

She gave him a look. "There are many things."

"Ah," he said, a half smile stretching his lips, "but you aren't one of them, remember?"

"I never said that."

"You didn't have to," he said, pushing past her into the house with a smile. Her heart flip-flopped as she smoothed her hand over her hair, insuring her face was covered. "I brought dinner."

A weird, unfamiliar feeling pulsed in her stomach. Like something was flying around in there and the winged thing also seemed to be affecting her heart. She wasn't sure she liked it. In fact, she was quite sure she didn't. What was happening to her? "Dinner?"

He gave her a look. "I assume you eat?"

She stared at him, baffled, as he put the bags on the counter and started to unpack the items.

"I'm not much of a cook," he said, "but I'm excellent at ordering take-out. We just need to warm this up."

He put the food in the microwave, then grabbed some plates from the cupboard and silverware from the drawers. It didn't go unnoticed that he seemed to know exactly where everything was, and she wondered how long he'd been awake the other morning and wandering around her house before he left. She had secrets, but they were all locked in her study with the glass orbs. There was no way he'd figured out how to get in there, she was certain of it.

"You seem to know your way around," she mused.

"You left me here alone. I used my time to try and find out more about you." He was honest and unapologetic.

"That sounds stalkery."

"Nope. I'm just a good investigator, and you're a lousy secret keeper."

She stiffened. "What do you mean?"

The microwave beeped and he pulled the container out, dropping it on the counter before doing a little hand dance to try and cool his fingers off. "I mean you probably shouldn't invite random strangers, especially incredibly attractive ones, into your house to stay the night. Clearly *I'm* not a threat, but you just probably shouldn't make it a habit. You know, 'for your own good'," he said, repeating the same line she'd used on him.

She fought a smile. "So it's okay if I invite unattractive random strangers to sleep over?"

He frowned. "Well you *could*, but I don't know why you'd want to." He paused, thinking, then pointed at her. "If you start making this stranger sleepover thing a habit, you should really call me so you have some back up."

She couldn't hold back her humor and the corners of her lips slid up. "Based on our previous adventure in the woods together, I don't really think I'm the one who needs to worry about defending myself."

He tilted his head in concession, a smile playing at the corner of his mouth as he handed her a plate and motioned for her to sit and eat. "Touché."

She looked him over, his dark jeans and green shirt much better camouflage than the neon yellow he'd been wearing the last time she'd seen him. "At least you had the fore-thought to wear something that would blend in this time."

He grinned at that. "Black doesn't really blend and it's all I've seen you wear."

"It blends when I go out. At night."

He studied her and she skirted his gaze, abruptly taking on an intense interest in the food he'd brought. Some sort of pasta concoction with a creamy sauce. It smelled delicious. He put a bag of warm breadsticks on the table and sat across from her.

"Where do you go when you go out at night?" Ledger asked.

She eyed him, knowing that answer would lead to questions about other things. She needed to bring up Bethany and her connection to his mom, but knew the conversation wouldn't be easy for him. "Your last name is Cross."

He nodded.

"I recognized it," she said, tasting her food. It was even better than it smelled. "Because of Bethany."

He paused, his fork half-way to his mouth. "My mom was a filmmaker. Documentaries mostly. Her work was popular with certain groups of people."

Jolie angled her head in acknowledgment. "I was a fan of

31

her films, but that's not why I recognized your name. I knew your mom."

He stared at her. "How?"

"She was a friend of mine. I met her because she knew the woman who raised me. Sola."

His mouth fell open and it took him several seconds to recover. "You're Sola's daughter?"

Jolie schooled her features, holding back her surprise at his recognition of Sola's name. Sola was powerful in the world of magic, and power births enemies. For her own safety, Sola had tried to stay under the radar and few people had access to her. The ones who did were the people who were deeply loyal and would never tell others about her. Bethany must have trusted Ledger immensely to give him Sola's information. "Biologically no, but in every other way. Sola had a lot of knowledge about things most people can't explain: the supernatural, energies, magic, other realms and beings. When Sola died, your mom started coming to me with questions. I don't have anywhere near the resources or knowledge that Sola did, but I helped when I could."

He stared at her, part shock, part excitement. "She'd been working on a documentary about the strange things that have happened in Withering Woods. Did you know about that?"

Jolie nodded. "I helped her with some of it. I'm very sorry for your loss. I miss seeing her."

He swallowed a lump in his throat, trying to deal with the emotion and randomness of being saved by this incredible warrior of the woods, and then finding out she knew his mom. "It was sudden. I'm still trying to deal with it."

She gave him a knowing look. "Grief is a different beast. It's something that never truly goes away; you just learn to live with the hole in your heart where the person used to be. The waves of emotion lose their strength over time, but they're still always lapping against the shore and occasionally they become a bigger storm. The emotional toll is over-whelming sometimes."

He looked at her then, holding her gaze. "Sola passed away four or five years ago. A stroke, right?"

Jolie nodded, putting her hands in her lap.

"I remember," he said, his voice softer. "My mom cried for days."

So had Jolie. Weeks passed, and then months. More than a year slogged by before she was ready to move forward and take up Sola's mantle of managing the odd occurrences of Withering Woods, and tracking down the ones who had hurt her and killed her parents. "Sola was an incredible woman. So was your mom."

He watched her closely as he said the next words, "My mom died near the spot where you helped me the other day."

She kept her face a neutral mask. He was testing her. "I know."

"I've been trying to find out what happened to her for two years. The only clue I had was the glass shattered around her." He held Jolie's gaze. "You have glass that looks almost identical in your library and upstairs."

Jolie stared at him, feeling violated and more than a little frustrated that he'd made it into a space she'd warded to insure no one would enter and if they did, she'd know it. On top of that, his interest in her now made sense. He hadn't come back because he wanted to be her friend, or because he'd somehow, inexplicably, found her attractive. He didn't think she was a skilled fighter of the supernatural. He'd seen the glass, recognized it, and drawn conclusions that she was somehow connected to his mom's death. He was there for answers, nothing more. Her demeanor turned icy. "You went in my study?"

"You left me here alone," he said, completely unapologetic.

"It was locked. And warded."

"You're not the only one who's been taught tricks."

She pressed her lips into a line and counted to ten to try and prevent herself from strangling him. When she calmed down, she answered, "Your mom had the glass orbs for protection. She was supposed to use them to contain some of the things that could hurt her in the woods."

He put his forearms on the table and leaned forward. "What things, exactly?"

"The same things that almost killed you the other night."

He leaned back in his chair, taking that in. "Do you know what happened to her?"

She took a deep breath. It wasn't easy to explain someone's last moments, but it was even harder when the deceased had been a friend and the person wanting answers had loved them deeply. "I didn't see the whole thing; I didn't get there in time. She'd been chased by the Screamers. They love things full of life. They're the reason the roses die each night in the woods; the Screamers wake at dusk and suck the life out of the flowers during the night. Sola always felt like the roses must carry something especially palatable to them —the equivalent of a sweet treat to a human. The Screamers hunt at night and feed off of the living. The more terrified their victim is, the more energy the Screamers get when they siphon a life. Your mom fell and when she did, the glass orb she had to contain them shattered. It was her only defense against the Screamers. I got to her after they'd already done their damage. I confined one of them and saw another fly off, but I couldn't save your mom." She paused, glancing at him; his eyes were bright with unshed tears. "She knew you'd come looking for her, Ledger. Her last words were asking me to keep you safe."

His entire body felt paralyzed, seized with emotion. A tear dropped onto his shirt, his chest tightening with the need to sob.

Jolie wanted to reach across the table and hug his pain away, but she didn't have the right. She needed to fulfill her promise to Bethany and keep him out of the woods. "You know what happened now; you don't need to keep searching."

He looked up at her, his eyes showing determination through his pain. She knew that look, it's what fueled her to hunt every night. But he didn't have the tools to do what she did. He could have a normal, happy life away from the realm of the unknown. That's what he needed, and she wasn't going to encourage him to continue searching the shadows. "If you keep trying to find what killed her, you're going to be in danger of the same thing happening to you."

He eyed her, confusion on his face before he scooted back, the chair making a scraping noise on the hardwood floor. "I need to go."

She nodded in understanding as he gathered his things. "I'm sorry, Ledger."

He stopped, his hand on the doorknob, but not turning around.

Jolie continued, "I thought you deserved to know."

He inclined his head once to the right, and then opened the door, leaving without another word.

She gave him a few minutes before silently following him to his car near the entrance of Withering Woods to make sure he got there without harm. She watched him drive away, convinced she'd never see him again.

Jolie returned to her house the next morning with more captures in one night than she'd ever had. One for every person she'd lost, including Ledger.

CHAPTER 4

$\mathcal{L}$ edger was a logical man who liked puzzles and mysteries. He enjoyed the process of trying to figure out the whys, hows, and motivations behind an event. He had approached his initial discovery of the glass in Jolie's house with the same logic. If she'd wanted to hurt him, she would have let him be taken by the shadow instead of defending him. She was hard to read, but she struck him as a protector, not someone who caused harm. The glass was an odd coincidence and he'd known there was a connection, he just hadn't been sure what. Maybe it was as simple as his mom finding the glass and breaking it when she fell. Or maybe there was a more detailed explanation and Jolie had the answers he was looking for.

He'd decided guessing was inefficient and pointless when he had the resource he needed right in the woods and he could ask her himself. Not to mention that it gave him an excuse to spend more time with her—something he'd been yearning for since the moment he met her. So it was with that path of logic that he'd ordered take-out and went back to Jolie's house.

She'd been stunning when she opened the door. Her thick hair a dark waterfall over the side of her face. He'd never been as captivated by a woman as he was by her. She was defiant and guarded, but an undercurrent of kindness ran through her and those things all combined to make him more intrigued. While he'd meant to get answers at dinner, he hadn't expected the conversation to go in the direction it had.

With her knowledge of the woods, Ledger had thought Jolie might know something about what had happened to his mom, or might at least be able to point him in the direction of where to look. He hadn't expected to find out Jolie had been there when his mom died. He always thought having answers would help him heal...make him more capable of moving on.

He was wrong.

Weeks passed and the empty spot in his soul stayed empty. He now knew it always would. It did not lessen his desire for vengeance, however. He had believed Jolie. Her account filled in the details that the police had never been able to—that his mom had been running from the fabled Screamers. That she'd fallen. And that a heart attack had nothing to do with her death. And the gouges on her arms and neck weren't from the fall, but something else entirely. Now that he knew the specifics, he was even more determined to find the thing that had taken his mom away from him, and kill it. But he couldn't do it alone. Luckily he knew the woman who could help him. And she looked spectacular in black.

It had been three weeks. Three sad weeks since Jolie had been on her first, and probably only, date. It's not like he'd actually asked her out, but it was the closest to a date she'd ever had, and the only time she'd eaten dinner with a man, let alone one who looked like a model, and made her heart pound and her stomach flutter.

When Ledger had shown up with dinner and that charming lopsided grin showcasing his perfect mouth, jawline, and...everything, really, she'd let her ridiculous dreams and romantic ideas run away with her. She'd found common ground with him discussing their losses and grief. She'd started painting a picture in her head of what it would be like to have a friend. She hadn't intended for things to go sideways, but when he'd brought up her glass orbs and made the connection with the broken shards around Bethany, she knew he hadn't brought her dinner because he wanted to see her. And even before he'd arrived, she'd already decided she needed to be honest with him and give him the truth about his mom. Jolie couldn't save Bethany, but she could at least try to help ease Ledger's pain. Given the way he'd left her that night, she didn't think she'd succeeded on that front.

And now she'd lost Ledger, someone she barely knew... someone she hadn't even realized she wanted.

Jolie trudged through the woods, her gait indicative of her thoughts. She hadn't been proficient at hunting lately, too caught up in her own head. So when she heard a noise behind her, she had to stop and really listen to decide if it was natural, or something else. She kept walking, paying more attention. She heard another snap, and then the crackle of leaves being stepped on. Someone—or something—was following her.

She knew the area, and knew where she could hide and wait for her pursuer. She moved quickly around a corner and then slid into a gash in the rock ahead that was invisible to the naked eye, and waited.

She didn't have to wait long.

She saw brown hiking boots first, covered by a pair of jeans that met a well-formed torso and familiar broad shoulders. Her heart started to race and her breath caught. Ledger. He was here. Again. But why? He knew what had happened to his mom. He had no reason to be back in the woods. And why was he following her? Maybe he didn't know it was her and he was out here on his own looking for the Screamers. She narrowed her eyes at the thought. If that was the case, she'd punch him.

He stopped like he was listening for something and looked around. He didn't seem to be finding it. Her romantic side got the best of her again, whispering that maybe the reason he'd come back was because he wanted to see her. She decided to test that theory, stepping out from the slash in the stone.

His eyes fell on her, taking her in with an emotion she couldn't identify. Relief? Appreciation? The first seemed ridiculous for someone who likely despised her for not being able to save his mom, and the second was even more absurd; no man had ever looked at her with any sort of interest, let alone appreciation.

"You were following me," she said. She stared at him, waiting for an explanation.

He bit the corner of his lip. "That sounds nefarious. I wasn't following—exactly. I've just been looking for you."

She crossed her arms over her chest and held his gaze. "So, stalking."

He pointed at her. "There's that nefarious sounding bit again."

"You know where I live, so why were you tracking me?"

He shrugged. "I tried your house, but you weren't there. I waited. You didn't come back. So I thought I'd try to find you."

She was more than displeased at his recklessness. "Considering you know what hunts people in these woods, I would think you'd know better."

"I came prepared," he said.

She was sure he thought he had. His mom had believed the same thing, and his mom had been given far more tools than he had. Jolie eyed him for several seconds and in that time, came to the conclusion that he was the most exasperating man she'd ever met—not that she'd met a lot—but she was certain even if she had, he'd still be at the top of her list. "I told you to stay away."

He eyed her. "I have authority issues." Half her face was covered by her hair again as the one turquoise eye he could see flashed with annoyance.

"You're infuriating," Jolie said through her teeth.

He nodded in concession. "Not the first time I've been accused of that."

"It doesn't surprise me in the least." She leaned against a tree trunk. "Why are you here?"

Ledger widened his stance, taking up far more space than she thought a person capable of in the middle of a wide open forest. "I want to talk to you."

She went completely still. "Why?"

"I need your help."

She stopped inhaling mid-breath and felt like she'd been punched. The romantic in her had been hoping for another explanation that started with something like: 'I can't stop thinking about you.' But this made much more sense. Ledger was here because he wanted her help. Last time he'd come with an offer of dinner in exchange for answers; this time he'd come for assistance. She closed her eyes, willing her heart to stop trying to influence her head. Someone as attractive as Ledger Cross would never want someone as broken and beastly as her. She needed to end the fantasies and delusions of romance, love, and happily ever afters that she'd fabricated in her mind. All hope for that was stolen from her years ago. She pushed aside the disappointment she felt at being needed instead of wanted—*desired*.

"I want to find the thing that murdered my mom, and I want to kill it."

He got right to the point. She appreciated his bluntness and brevity. But she also wouldn't help him on his potential suicide mission. The Screamers were not something to be messed with. She shook her head and pushed off from the tree, walking away. "No."

"No?" he asked, his voice incredulous. "Do you want to explain your decision?"

She shook her head and started following a path covered with smooth rocks. "Not really."

She could hear the crunch of the rocks moving under his shoes as he trailed behind her. Stealth was not something he seemed to be acquainted with, unsurprising given his size. His lack of covertness wouldn't help him reach his goals, and would likely get him killed.

"You know I'm going to do this, with or without you, right?" His tone was harsher, more determined.

She winced. "I was worried you'd say that."

"So will you help me?"

She stopped, turned, and took him in. Every part of his being was a study in perfection. He should be living a happy, carefree life, far away from the woods and the dangers that lived here. His jaw was set with resolve and she shook her head slowly in answer.

"Why? I at least deserve to know that."

She squared her shoulders and lifted her gaze to his. "Because when your mom was sprawled on the ground, taking her last breaths, the only words she was able to mutter were to ask me to keep you safe. She knew you'd try to find out what had happened to her, and she knew it would be dangerous. Leading you into a fight that might end the same way Bethany's did does not honor her final request."

He watched her, thinking through her statement. "She might have asked you to watch out for me, which means she trusted you a great deal. But she never would have told me not to fight. That's what I intend to do. They took my mom. I won't let them take a loved one from someone else—not when I have the ability to do something about it. While I respect your decision, it doesn't change my plans."

She assessed him, listening to his argument. His points were good, and he stood a better chance with a partner. But she wasn't sure she should be it, for a multitude of reasons—the biggest one being her heart. It was selfish and cowardly, but it was true. "I respect your decision as well."

Ledger pressed his lips into a line as he nodded in response, and then pulled the backpack off his shoulder. He put it on the ground and crouched down, opening the zipper. "I brought you something." He pulled out a rectangular item wrapped in a deep metallic green paper, and handed it to her.

She gave him a skeptical look. "I don't need a gift."

He watched her, his lips sliding into that slow, hypno-tizing grin. "I'm hoping this means you prefer physical touch since gifts *clearly* aren't your love language."

She folded her arms across her chest. "That's not funny." She'd read the love languages book. She knew what they were…even though the knowledge was pointless since she had no use for love or its various dialects.

"It wasn't meant to be funny," Ledger answered. An awkward silence fell between them and he scrubbed a hand over his jaw, his stubble rustling with the movement. "Look, I just wanted to say thank you. For talking to me about my mom and helping me get the answers I needed. You didn't have to share the information, but you did, and you were kind. The details were important to helping me move forward. Thank you. And I also wanted to thank you for the day we met in the woods...for helping me."

She raised a brow. "You mean *saving* you?"

He tilted his head in agreement. "Okay. I'm not too prideful to admit that. You saved me. Thank you."

She gave him a considering look.

"And," he said, stuffing his hands in his pockets, his eyes searching the ground, "even if you don't want to help me find the Screamers, I still want to get to know you better."

Her heart felt like it stopped. If not stopped, at least skipped several beats. Those words were things she'd been wanting to hear from a man her whole life. A dream she thought she'd never have realized. But she couldn't help questioning where the urge came from. Was it because she'd known his mom and he wanted to hear more about Jolie's relationship with her? Was it because he still held out hope for her help? Or, by some miracle, was it because he actually had some kind of interest in her beyond her knowledge and potential assistance. She immediately shook that off. No. That couldn't be it. And even if it was, he didn't know about what had happened to her. He hadn't seen her scars. If he had, he wouldn't want to know her better. She was certain of it. She hated being vulnerable and there was nothing more vulnerable than the heart. She wasn't willing to risk the pain that would come from his rejection.

Leaving was far easier than opening up her heart to the unknown. "No," she said, using the heel of her boot to turn and start to walk away.

He sidestepped to stand in front of her. "Why?"

"Because I don't like people."

He narrowed his eyes. "You don't like people, or you don't like me?"

"Both."

He eyed her speculatively. "I'd like the chance to change your mind."

She stepped around him to leave. "You won't get it."

"I'm not an easy man to discourage."

She frowned. "I've noticed."

"You can walk away," he said, his voice unwavering, "but know that I'll come back."

"I wish you wouldn't," she shot back over her shoulder.

He gave her a look like he knew better and she had the fleeting thought that maybe he did. This man might see her heart more clearly than she saw it herself. The thought was terrifying.

She escaped Ledger and then quietly followed him like she always did when she knew he was wandering the woods alone, listening for any predators until he was safely past the rose arch entrance. She'd scouted earlier and hadn't seen anything, but she could never be completely sure. She waited until she heard his car door shut before she looked at the gift in her hand, a combination of excitement and wariness washing over her. She hadn't been given a gift in years. Jolie turned the present over, and slowly started to unwrap the emerald paper. He was right, gifts weren't her love language, but she'd also never been given one by someone other than Sola. His thoughtfulness made her heart constrict.

She gently lifted the paper off of the item and stared. It was a copy of the last book in her favorite series…the series she'd just finished rereading to prepare for the last book. She had the final copy on her eReader, but hadn't yet bought it in print to complete the collection for her library. She opened the novel, taking joy in the first lift of the cover, the smell of fresh paper and ink on crisp pages, and the slight creak of the spine as the hardcover weighed down one side. She flipped past the title page and immediately gasped.

The book was signed. Personalized to Jolie with a note from the author.

Her breath caught and a lump formed in her throat as tears pricked her eyes. He'd noticed her books. He'd noted her favorite series. And he'd seen she was missing one. Then he'd gone out of his way to not only get it for her, but figure out how to get it signed. It was a thoughtful, detailed gesture, and more than that, it was kind.

She wasn't used to kindness.

CHAPTER 5

*J*olie didn't trust people. She had a long list of reasons why, all completely legit. The fact that she'd had no friends growing up, and the few times she had interacted with people hadn't gone well, didn't help the situation. It was easier to be alone than to be at someone's mercy. She'd learned a long time ago that the only person you can truly rely on is yourself. There had been one exception. Sola, her adopted mom. She'd taken Jolie in as a baby and raised her as her own. She'd been a mother to Jolie, and Jolie would be forever grateful for it. She'd home-schooled Jolie, and in addition to her core subject lessons, she'd taught Jolie everything she needed to know to survive in Withering Woods and the world of the inconceivable. When Sola died from a stroke five years ago, Jolie made peace with the fact that she was, and always would be, alone.

The only other people she'd had contact with were people who had known Sola and consulted with her for her skills. Bethany was one of them, and she'd made a point to continually check in on Jolie after Sola died. Jolie's heart held a special place for Bethany—for constantly making sure she was okay after her loss, for being a friend, and for not pitying her for her circumstances.

So by proxy, that meant Bethany's son held a special place as well. Jolie pursed her lips, thinking, and not liking what she found. If she was being honest with herself, it wasn't just because he was Bethany's son that he held a special place in her heart. She cared for him in a way she'd never cared for anyone else. A way she hadn't allowed herself to even dream of caring. A way she wasn't comfortable with. If she let her feelings manifest, she knew it wouldn't end well and she'd lose another person from her life. She could handle being alone. She just wasn't prepared for how much she liked having someone in her life.

She'd analyzed her feelings and actions a lot since Ledger had left her with his gift. The thought of making herself vulnerable and letting another person in terrified her. It was one of the main reasons she'd said no when Ledger asked her for help finding and killing the Screamers who took his mom. But she'd been through hell and back, and she prided herself on being fearless. She wasn't about to let fear start making choices for her now.

She'd promised Bethany she would watch over Ledger. By not helping him and letting him go off into the woods on his own, she wasn't honoring Bethany's wishes either. If he was determined to do this, he needed someone who knew the woods like the back of their hand, and someone who knew their opponent better than any other. There was no one better qualified for this situation than Jolie. Her decision was made.

She went to her room, taking the piece of paper out of her drawer that he'd left her that first night he'd stayed at her house. Her fingers held it gently like a treasured object. For someone who thought she had no one, that paper, that number, and that connection, was more valuable than gold.

She thumbed his number into her phone and then sent him a text.

My house. Tonight. 7.

She quickly realized that sounded a lot like an invitation for something more than hunting in the woods, but before she could respond, he already had.

It sounds like a date. Also, who is this?

"Dang it," she hissed. She didn't text much and she obviously needed some tutoring. She quickly texted back.

Jolie.

Then I'm even happier for the invitation.

Her stomach did that odd flip-flopping thing again that she always read about in novels but had never experienced herself. That wasn't good. Keeping her feelings in check was the only way their partnership could last. She needed to set expectations up front. Even if he was interested in her, any feelings he might have would be fleeting. She needed to help him accomplish his goals. Nothing more. And then maybe when it was all over, they could still be friends. She typed back.

It's not a date.

It's kind of a date.

You need to be trained.

I'm a good student. I'm an even better date.

We're not dating.

Not yet.

She glared at the screen. This wouldn't do at all. As soon as he arrived tonight, they were going to have a discussion about working relationships.

Her commitment to the no dating rule she'd established in her head lasted until she opened the door to find Ledger looking all Adonis-y and holding dinner in one hand again, and bright, beautiful fuchsia roses in the other.

"Why can't the Screamers leave the woods?" Ledger asked as they moved along a path thick with trees. They'd been hunting for a while and it was all he could do to pay attention to what Jolie was saying instead of watching her. She moved with the grace of a dancer and the eyes of a predator. She was strong, smart, and striking in a way no other woman he'd ever met before had been. And she had no idea how beautiful she was.

"The woods are full of all kinds of magic and things that most people don't believe in." She crossed a stream hopping from rock to rock. Ledger followed. "It's not just the Screamers who stay in the forest; it's all paranormal beings. And it's not that they can't leave, they just prefer not to."

He pushed his brows together. "Why?"

She lifted a shoulder. "It's easier for them here."

"Why is that?" he asked again.

She gave him a considering look then tilted her head toward the north. "Come on, I'll show you."

She veered off the path and he followed her, climbing through overgrown bushes and dodging trees and boulders. The area was not well-traveled by humans and they were no longer following any sort of trail. He was certain she was leading him on a wild goose chase and playing some kind of joke...until they came to a wide clearing. White rocks were scattered amid soil and trees. She bent down, picking up a handful of dirt. The dirt glittered with white specks in the sunlight. "Quartz."

She could practically see the connections clicking together in his mind. With his background in the unexplained, he should already have an understanding of the power of gemstones.

"Quartz is known for its ability to absorb and release

energy," she said, dropping the dirt and standing back up. "The crystal acts as a conductor for all things supernatural. It bridges the gap between our world and other realms. Most of the paranormal beings in this area can harness it for power, and replenish their power from it. So while they *can* leave, there's no reason to when they're that close to a source of limitless energy."

Ledger looked out over the sea of quartz. "I've heard of this happening in other places," he said, running his hand over a piece of bright white rock. "People in the paranormal fields have speculated that energy has a lot to do with locations where there are high concentrations of the unexplained."

Jolie nodded. "Fairy mounds, standing stones, gemstones, crystals, water, fire—the list is endless. Everything is energy and when you realize that, it becomes easier to harness the elements and the various powers available. Energy is something supernatural beings know a hell of a lot more about than we do, and they use the knowledge to their advantage."

"If location and energy is so important, then why do we have sightings of paranormal beings all over the world and not just in locations with a high concentration of energy? If the energy is so readily available in those areas, why would paranormal beings ever leave?" Ledger asked.

She shifted her bag from her back and unzipped it, pulling out two bottled waters and handing Ledger one. "It's not like they can't leave. It's just easier to stay. They're like us, only much longer lived. They've been around for eons. They get bored and like to try new places and see new things. But most of them will move from one energy source location to another in order to maintain their power."

He shifted his weight and looked up through the trees. "How long have the Screamers been here?"

The plastic seal on her water cap made a popping noise as

she cracked it open and took a drink. "Probably longer than people have."

Ledger brought his attention back to her. "But they're supposed to feed off the power of the living. How did they survive before humans came into existence? Plants? Animals?"

She shook her head at his misconception. "The Screamers don't *need* to siphon life to live. They can easily get power from the quartz. But they have no conscience and no sense of compassion. They don't care if they kill. For them it's something to do that they've turned into a game. If they win the game—which they usually do—they get more power from it. There's no reason for them not to do it."

He gave her an incredulous look. "So they kill people just to be jerks?"

"Pretty much."

He sat down on a rock. He'd spent years helping his mom research things that most people didn't believe existed. He thought he knew a lot, but talking with Jolie it was clear he hadn't even scratched the surface. He had a plethora of questions and he was grateful Jolie had so many answers. "How do the Screamers reproduce?"

Her lips ticked up and she gave him a rare smile. He liked it. A lot. He wanted to make it happen again and again. "If you're asking me to give you the birds and the bees talk, it's not going to happen."

He gave her a look. "I'm serious."

She pushed her brows together. "I don't know for sure. How do most paranormal beings come into existence? It's a mystery. I've always had a theory about the Screamers, though, and Sola thought my hypothesis was feasible. I've seen Screamers split in two before while fighting. I've often wondered if they multiply that way."

He ran his tongue over the inside of his cheek, mulling

her idea over. "So they could be multiplying in the orbs once you've captured them?"

While she'd given Ledger an overview of the orbs when she was telling him about what happened to his mom, she'd explained them in depth before she agreed to let him hunt with her. He'd committed the containment spell to memory, and knew to carry at least one orb any time he was in the woods. She had spelled weapons that could slow the Screamers down, but next to warding and protection spells, the orbs were the only way to stop the Screamers, and one of the only defenses a human had. The orbs were their most powerful weapon. Sola had been an expert in the orbs, and had spent years learning to manipulate glass to make them. She'd taught Jolie, but Jolie wasn't nearly as skilled as Sola had been. Her orb making ability was something Jolie constantly tried to improve on, but she felt like there were things she still didn't know and she often wished she could ask Sola for answers. As she considered Ledger's question, she realized this was one of those times. "I guess it's technically possible, but even if they *are* multiplying, once they're in the orbs they're trapped."

Ledger bit the corner of his lip. "If they split enough times, wouldn't they get big enough that the orbs couldn't hold them anymore?"

She thought about it some more, and again wished for Sola's guidance. "I honestly don't know. I've never had it happen before though, and I still have orbs locked away from Sola's first captures over forty years ago."

He gave her a look. "It might be something you want to look into."

She nodded in agreement. "I'll do that." Maybe she could find some information about it in one of Sola's journals.

Ledger started to ask another question when they were abruptly interrupted by a cry that sounded like nails on a chalkboard. Ledger's head jerked to the right and left, then up, trying to figure out where the noise was coming from. Jolie swore under her breath at her carelessness. She should have known better than to linger in one of the quartz clearings. Supernatural beings were always in the area. Two shadows swooped down on them. Jolie's eyes shot to Ledger. She'd been doing this for years. He hadn't. Her immediate instinct was to save him before herself. She pulled an orb from her bag and rushed toward him, holding the glass ball out in front of her as she spoke the spell that would contain the Screamers and stop them from hurting her friend.

As her words grew louder, the screams grew more shrill. The sound of the spell was painful to the Screamers, as was the physical transition that took place for them to shift into the orb. They turned toward Jolie, their glowing amber and indigo eyes radiating ire. She wasn't concerned. She'd dealt with this before. The spell held them captive and she was finishing the words that would imprison them when she saw another shadow swoop in from the left. Her heart started pounding, a hammer in her chest, and she sped up her words. She had to finish this spell and contain the two Screamers already there or she'd end up having to deal with all of them at once. The more Screamers there were, the harder they were to contain, especially without preparation.

Ledger saw them coming and held up a crystal of his own. It must have been spelled with something, because it flashed a bright, disorienting light, and repelled the Screamer. She didn't think the stun would last long, however.

She was right. The Screamer flew back at Ledger, doubling his speed. Jolie sped through the last lines of her spell as the two Screamers in front of her were sucked into the orb, subdued. She turned in time to see Ledger grappling with the other Screamer. Ledger was on the ground, fighting, his crystal several feet away and shattered like it had been violently thrown. The Screamer was above him, its hands a shadowy thief stealing his breath. It was the same position his mom had been in when Jolie couldn't save her.

"No!" Jolie screamed, running toward the shadow. She unsheathed a spelled knife from a belt on her leg and threw it at the Screamer. The knife wouldn't stop the shadow, but it would slow it down. The knife sliced straight through the middle of the Screamer and it let out a yelp of pain. Puce colored liquid oozed from the slice. The shadow flew toward Jolie, knocking her down. She yanked her necklace off, the string becoming three times as long now that it was uncoiled. She whipped it over her head like a lasso and caught the shadow. It used all of its strength to fight against her, but that was nothing compared to Jolie's skill and training. She used the necklace to drag the Screamer back over to the orb she'd left on the ground, then spoke the words of the containment spell, the being wailing as it was pulled inside with the others. Holding the orb in one hand and her necklace in the other, she closed her eyes and breathed a sigh of relief it was over. Ledger was fine—she'd seen his chest rising and falling—and she'd gotten to him in time. Everything was okay.

But when she opened her eyes, she knew she'd been wrong about that. Everything was *not* okay. Ledger was standing in front of her, his eyes wide, a familiar look of horror covering his expression as he stared. "Jolie...your face."

She inhaled sharply.

He'd seen her scars.

He knew she was a monster.

CHAPTER 6

"What happened?" Ledger asked, gently.

She put the orbs in her bag, securing it over her shoulders, and turned away from him, her back as effective of a curtain as her hair. It hid her emotions: embarrassment for what she looked like, hatred for the beings who had done it to her, who had taken so much from her, and were now about to take again. Ledger would want nothing to do with her after this. Tears pricked her eyes and she fought them back, swallowing hard as she bent to retrieve her knife. She sheathed it in the holder on her thigh and when she was certain she had control again, she turned back around to face him. "I've never fought them so close to their quartz power source. I suspect it gave them an advantage."

He held her gaze, his voice soft as he carefully said, "I wasn't talking about the fight, Jolie."

She knew that. But she was hoping he'd have the sense not to ask for more details. She'd never fought with anyone who didn't know about her past before. She didn't even think of needing to take precautions to make sure her scars didn't show during battle. It was her own fault he knew her secret.

ANGELA CORBETT

She started walking away, back to the house, an empty feeling settling deep in her soul. She heard his footsteps following behind her. She watched the skies and their surroundings vigilantly as they walked, paying closer attention than she had been earlier. They'd already had one incident, they didn't need another. She'd be more cognizant of the quartz and stay away from fights in the area in the future.

She berated herself the entire way back home, trying to figure out how she'd explain things to him. Maybe it would be better to leave well enough alone. He didn't need an explanation. He wouldn't be back. He'd leave her tonight without a word and she'd haunt his nightmares instead of his dreams. The injustice of it made her want to yell and punch things. She took some cleansing breaths to calm down. This was her reality...one she accepted long ago. It was no different than it had always been except that for a while, one of her dreams of being treated like a normal woman had actually been a reality. She'd known it wouldn't last from the beginning, and she should have been better prepared for this moment. She would cling to the memories and use them as a crutch during the bad times.

They got back to the house and she opened the door, making her way up the stairs to the study where she locked the orbs in the spelled glass case. She took another deep breath before going down the stairs to face what she was certain would be an empty house. He would have left as soon as he had the chance, and she didn't blame him.

Her breath caught with surprise and a bloom of traitorous hope when she hit the bottom step and saw him leaning against the wall, thick forearms crossed over his chest, waiting for her.

"You're still here," she said, stating the obvious.

He lifted his brows. "Did you think I wouldn't be?"

Of course he was still here. It was nighttime. He knew

better than to go out in the woods at night if he didn't have to. "That's good. It's not safe out there. I can follow you to your car though so you can leave." So he could get away from her.

He gave her a look. "I'm not here because I'm worried about my safety, Jolie."

She didn't want to ask why he was still there...yet she desperately wanted to ask why he was still there.

"What happened to you?" Ledger asked again, his tone soft and concerned.

She couldn't meet his gaze. "It doesn't matter. It was a long time ago."

He reached for her and she immediately backed away, re-smoothing the curtain of hair over her face.

A muscle ticked at his temple and his jaw was set in a determined line. "I don't care if it happened a week ago or twenty years ago. I want to know you, Jolie. I want you to let me in."

She stared at him, dumbfounded. For a minute, she actually believed him. Believed he was invested in more than her knowledge, and he wasn't just using her to help in his quest for vengeance. But no, that couldn't be true. No one would care for someone who looked like she did, who had the baggage she had. She was a mess and this man, who was perfect in every way, deserved someone just as incredible. She wasn't it. She'd built armor around her heart for years—it was the only way to protect herself. She couldn't simply drop it and let him in; armor doesn't dissolve that way. It didn't matter what he said to her, the story she'd told herself about her scars, about how people perceived her, was stronger than his words.

She could feel the tears start to well and knew her emotions were about to flood her cheeks. She'd already been humiliated enough and couldn't handle him seeing any more of her weakness tonight. Still holding her bag, she swung it over her shoulder, opened the front door, and she ran.

Six hours later Jolie stomped back up her porch, her mood foul. She'd been angry when she left: furious with herself, with life, and with the cards she'd been dealt. She'd needed a good pity party and she'd used every ounce of anger as fuel to kill. She'd destroyed a lot of Screamers in an attempt to assuage her resentment and temper. It hadn't made her feel better.

She opened the front door. She knew Ledger would be gone. She'd been surprised he'd followed her back to the house earlier, and had wanted to talk to her about her scars. He should have run away like every other person who had ever seen her face. It was early morning and daylight again. He was safe and could have left on his own without her as backup hours ago. She'd stayed out hunting longer on purpose just so he'd have the chance to leave without it being awkward between them. She thought about what her days would look like now—a lot like they had for years before Ledger came into her life. She'd go back to hunting at night, reading in her library during the day, and she'd try to forget about what might have been.

She walked in the house with her bag slung over her shoulder and started up the stairs. She glanced at the living room on her way up the steps, and froze.

Ledger was still there. Sitting on her couch.

Jolie blinked.

Still there.

She blinked again, certain he was a mirage.

"I'm still here. You can stop blinking," Ledger said.

She moved her bag from her shoulder and carefully put it

on the floor, eying him with suspicion. "*Why* are you still here?"

"Because I was worried about you." His eyes were clear, his expression honest, and his concern completely confused her.

"I'm fine. I've been doing this every night for years."

He looked at her the way someone looks at a wounded animal they're trying to approach and help. "We were attacked in the woods by things that weren't human, and then you refused to talk to me. I wasn't just worried about your physical safety, Jolie. I was worried about your emotional health."

She pressed her lips into a line before saying again, "I'm fine."

His eyes widened. "Are you? Because you ran instead of talking to me. If you don't want to discuss what happened to you, I understand. But the fact that you ran tells me there's more to it than just not wanting to talk. I told you I want to get to know you. I want to be there for you." His voice took on a pleading tone. "Let me be there for you."

Her heart felt like someone was squeezing it violently. She sunk down onto one of steps on her stairway, face in her hands. She couldn't believe this was happening. That he was still here, that he'd seen her scars and hadn't regarded her with the same revulsion she'd received in the past. Maybe he really did care about her and want to know her. She wasn't ready to shuck her armor, but maybe it was time for her to take some pieces off. It was a risk. There was no guarantee he'd stay even after she told him what happened. But she knew the outcome of not letting people in; perhaps it was time to try another path.

She took a deep breath and moved her hands from her face. She knew she couldn't meet his eyes and tell the story, so she focused on a knot in the hardwood floor. "I was six. I was in Withering Woods, camping with my parents. They knew the rumors about the forest and that people shouldn't stay through the night, but they thought the warnings were just stories, urban legends passed down to scare teenagers." Her eyelids fluttered closed, trying to block the repressed images from invading her consciousness. "We'd been there three nights when the Screamers came. There were five of them. Knowing what I know about the Screamers now, I think they'd been watching us since we arrived. They surrounded us while we were sitting around the fire, roasting marshmallows. My parents had no idea what they were, or how to defend against them." She paused, the memory like a horror scene being acted out in front of her all over again. "They took my dad first. He was on the ground and dead within seconds. Then they went after me and my mom. She tried to protect me as the Screamers surrounded us both. One of them was larger than the others. I remember because it had bright yellow eyes. To this day, I've never seen another Screamer with eyes like that. He's the Screamer who killed my dad, and then grabbed my mom, throwing her to the ground. She yelled for me to run but I couldn't leave her. I stayed and tried to fight them off. The other Screamers pushed me back, slashing at me and leaving claw marks down the side of my face and neck. I heard my mom yelling in pain and knew something awful was happening to her, but I couldn't help her. And I knew in my soul that the same thing was about to happen to me. But suddenly the Screamers were gone. It was Sola. She contained three of them, but the other two, including the one with yellow eyes, flew off."

Ledger tried to process everything she'd said. He'd lost his mom, but he couldn't even begin to understand what Jolie must have gone through. She'd lost both her parents right in front of her eyes, and she blamed herself for not being able to help them more. And then she'd lost Sola. Everyone in her life who she'd ever loved was gone. The loneliness and sadness must be devastating. He moved tentatively toward her, crouching down in front of her, putting his hand on her knee in a gesture of comfort. "Losing a parent would be a horrible thing to go through at any age, but especially that young. I'm so sorry for your loss, Jolie. And I'm sorry you had to experience a physical and emotional trauma like that."

She nodded a thank you, but still couldn't meet his eyes. "The Screamers were responsible for the attack. But the one specific yellow-eyed demon was responsible for killing my parents. I've been hunting that Screamer for years."

He looked at her, his eyes showing an understanding. Jolie recognized the need for justice and she knew what he was going through in regard to his own mom.

"Did Sola adopt you?" he asked.

She gave a slight shake of her head. "Not legally, but she was my mom in every way that mattered. Sola saved me. She took me back to the house that night, dressed my wounds, and healed me using her spells. But even her extensive knowledge of magic couldn't stop the scars. She always blamed herself for that, but it wasn't her fault. Without her, I would have been dead. I was alive, and that's what mattered. Sola kept me with her and raised me as her own. I owed her my life and I was happy I got to spend so much time with her before she died."

His eyes shined, wet with empathy and understanding. "That's a lot of loss for someone so young."

She shrugged. "We all have our issues. Everyone suffers in one way or another and has to learn to deal with it."

He considered her for a minute before answering. "I went through a loss like yours as an adult and it took me years to get over it. I'm still not, and I know I never will be. That's not how grief works. You had to deal with it as a child, times two, and the scars—emotional and physical—that came with it. Then you dealt with it again as an adult." He took her hands in his and a pulse ran through his whole body. "You should wear your scars like the trophy they are, Jolie. You earned those marks because you weren't afraid to fight and try to save your family. And you were a child at the time. You're one of the strongest, bravest people I've ever met."

It was the first time anyone had ever seen her scars as a battle wound that should be celebrated. She'd never looked at them like that. A thrill of pride ran through her at the difference in perspective. Her scars might be a component of who she was, but they didn't define her. They were a visual representation of her willingness to fight, protect, and never give up. He was right, and she should be proud of that.

"Don't belittle your battle by convincing yourself to be ashamed of your appearance. You're beautiful, Jolie. The scars make you even more so."

She blushed, tears welling in her eyes. He said she was beautiful. She thought he might really mean it. No one had ever called her beautiful before.

He leaned in, placing his hand on her cheek. His lips were soft butterfly wings fluttering in front of hers, about to make contact. Her heart felt like it would pound right through her chest.

"No," she said, pulling back. She didn't want the kiss. Not like this. She'd seen the sadness in his eyes as she told him her story. He was kissing her to try and make her feel better, not because he wanted to.

He pulled back, searching her eyes, realization setting in. "It's not pity you're seeing, Jolie. It's heartbreak. For what happened to you. For what you had to endure physically, as well as emotionally. I can't imagine, and my heart breaks for you for that. But I would *never* pity you. You're one of the bravest people I know. I *admire* you."

They were pretty words, and she wanted to trust that they were true, but she couldn't. It's difficult to overwrite history and believe the good when you've only been shown the bad. "I wish I could believe you."

He held her gaze. "I'm going to do everything in my power to prove it to you."

CHAPTER 7

$\mathcal{L}$ edger hadn't been making false promises. Despite Jolie's initial hesitation and disbelief that he'd even come back, he did. Every night. Over the course of the next few months, Ledger went out with her in the woods and they hunted the Screamers, looking specifically for one with bright yellow eyes.

After they got home from hunting, they would take their glass orbs to her study to be locked away. Sometimes they would talk, other times they would read together or watch a movie. Often she would fall asleep on his shoulder, and the two of them would wake up, a tangle of entwined limbs. Those were her favorite moments.

Slowly Jolie started to trust him more, and over time, even started to rely on him—something she hadn't allowed herself to do since Sola died. She'd been alone for years, and thought she always would be. Self-sufficiency was paramount. But Ledger had taught her she could be strong and even better with a partner. She had a companion for the first time, and she realized how much that meant to her.

Gradually, she became less and less aware of the placement of her hair around Ledger. He already knew her secret and it hadn't scared him away. It mystified her, but he truly seemed to respect her more for her scars. It felt incredible to have a partner, a friend, and someone she could be herself with.

The night was dark, the moon a slight sliver in the sky. On their patrols during the past week, they'd found a nest of Screamers staying in an area deep in the woods. The two of them had tracked the Screamers, then spent days figuring out the best plan of attack. Tonight they were going to implement it. They were each wearing their backpacks with containment orbs, and they both had backup orbs just in case. Jolie and Ledger planned to strike from two sides, forcing the Screamers into the middle so they could each pull as many of the ethereal shadows into the orbs as possible at once. If something went wrong, one of them could stop reciting the spell and help the other one.

They reached the edge of the nest where they'd have to split to move into position. "Okay, just like we practiced," Jolie whispered, her heart racing. She didn't usually get nervous, but this was an entire nest of Screamers and it wasn't just her safety to consider. They'd planned and planned, and were as prepared as they could be. She had to trust that. "You go in on the left, I'll go on the right. We'll start saying the spell in tandem and that should give us the power we need to get them all." The breeze picked up, lifting the hair off her face. She'd been parting it this way for so long that it was like it had its own muscle memory. He'd already seen her scars repeatedly but she smoothed her hand down trying to tame it anyway, an involuntary reaction built on years of habit.

Ledger reached up and moved her hair away from her face, caressing the battered skin like it was a rare jewel. To him, it was. "We'll be fine."

She closed her eyes and inhaled a deep breath. Fighting otherworldly beings was always a risk. One she was even less inclined to take when it wasn't just her life on the line. She released a rattled exhale, trying to calm down.

He lifted her chin, forcing her eyes to meet his. "Do you know your name means 'pretty' in French?"

She did. She'd always thought it was a cruel twist of fate that her parents had given her such a lovely name when her beauty had been taken from her. She nodded slightly in answer to his question.

"It's the perfect name for the perfect girl."

Her eyes fluttered as she looked up at him, part shock, part disbelief.

His expression turned playful, his irises sparkling. "When we beat the Screamers, I think we should get a reward."

Her brows shifted up. "Oh really?"

He licked his lips. "Uh huh."

"What kind of a reward?"

He leaned down, his mouth a hairsbreadth from hers, his voice husky, "The kind that's worth waiting for. And I think we've waited almost long enough."

Her cheeks immediately felt hot. They'd held hands, fallen asleep together, and had genuine affection for one another, but they hadn't kissed yet—she'd evaded him each time they'd gotten close. Not because she didn't want to kiss him. She wanted it more than anything. But she had to be certain Ledger was doing it for the right reasons. And frankly, she was a little nervous. She'd never kissed a man, and it's not like she'd ever taken a kissing class. She watched a lot of movies and read a lot of books, so that helped, but still. A first kiss was a big deal. It wasn't something you could do over. She wanted it to be perfect.

He kissed her on her still pink cheeks. "Be careful, beautiful girl. I'll see you soon."

She managed to hold her huge smile in until he was walking away, but he turned around and caught it, then flashed her a wide grin of his own. For the first time in her life, she could honestly say she was happy. She hoped it would never end.

The hope was short lived, however, as their attack didn't go quite as planned. Ledger came in from the side on cue at the same time as Jolie. They were both holding their orbs and started the containment spell immediately. It was working at first, but then for some reason the orb she'd been holding shattered, and with it, some of their power was lost. Before Jolie could get another orb from her pack, she was accosted from behind by a Screamer.

She elbowed at the demon, trying to get it off of her. She pulled her knife from the sheath wrapped around her thigh and sliced at her attacker. It yelled, and paused its attack long enough for Jolie to reach in her pack. Then the Screamer was back on her, whipping at her shoulders and spine. Jolie grabbed an orb from her bag and fought the demon. She started the spell and spun around, but froze when she saw the Screamer that held her. It had glowing, bright yellow eyes.

Anger bubbled in her chest—a cauldron of emotion and pure hatred. This was the entity responsible for killing her parents and helping to maim her. She wanted nothing more than to rip it apart. She reached for her special spelled sword instead of the orb she'd been holding. She was furious, and unwilling to give it a quick and easy death. "I've been looking for you," she told the yellow-eyed monster. She'd always believed her scars made her beastly, but now realized her appearance had nothing to do with it. It's not what a person looks like that makes them a beast; it's their actions, choices, and how they treat others. This fiend who had taken her parents and ruined her life was the definition of a monster.

"I've been looking for you, too," the Screamer drawled out in a deep voice, the words slurred together like it hadn't opened its mouth all the way and was trying to speak through its teeth.

Sola had told her the Screamers could speak, but she'd never actually heard one. It was a jarring experience and she hated the thing even more after hearing its gruff voice. Her eyes darted to Ledger. He was still saying the spell, and holding his own against the Screamers near him. She was grateful he was okay and didn't need help at the moment because she didn't have the power or focus to offer.

The Screamer's eyes followed hers. "How sweet," the monster said. "The two parentless children found each other." Its voice was like rocks being ground against pavement. "I remember when I killed your parents," it said. "I always regretted you got away. Not unharmed though, I see. That's good. You've been hunting and killing my kind for years. It's time for me to return the favor."

Fury coursed through her. This beast that so casually took life and found strength in causing pain didn't deserve to live. She was going to make sure he didn't. "I don't think so," she said, taking her sword and slashing it across the Screamer's stomach. It shot backward, doubling over in pain. After some time, it slowly lifted its head. "A spelled blade. Smart. It's the only smart thing you've done. You will die tonight." Its attention drifted to Ledger. "And so will he."

The threat of having yet another person she cared about taken by this beast turned her fury white hot. Her eyes were shooting daggers as the corner of her lips ticked up, antagonizing. "Bring it on, you stupid Mothman wannabe."

The yellow light of its eyes flashed. "So much ego. I wonder if you'll still have it when I tell you my secret."

She eyed him closely, fully aware that he was trying to throw her off her game.

He purred the words with pride, "I killed his mom, too."

Jolie gasped, losing concentration as her gaze searched for Ledger, wondering if he'd heard the yellow-eyed Screamer's admission. Could it be true? Jolie hadn't gotten there in time to see the entire scene or how many Screamers had been in the vicinity. She had contained one and saw another fly off, but she never saw its face. The yellow-eyed monster could have killed Bethany, and if that was the case, Jolie had even more reason to hate it and want it dead. She was distracted with her thoughts and didn't move out of the Screamer's way in time. It tackled her to the ground, growling and slashing. "I hope you cry just like your parents did," it said. Her sword had fallen when she was tackled. She patted her hands around in the dirt, searching for it, or one of her other forms of defense—anything to slow the Screamer down.

The Screamer's finger-like tendrils were circling her neck, getting tighter with each passing second. She was going to choke to death before he even got the chance to take her life force—something she counted as a blessing. But right before she passed out, the weight was lifted from her, the grip on her neck loosening.

Her eyes fluttered open but she'd been without oxygen for so long she questioned whether everything she was seeing was an illusion. She saw Ledger standing there, her sword in his hand. "This is for my mom," he growled, slashing the yellow-eyed Screamer repeatedly across the neck. "And this is for Jolie's parents," he said, stabbing the sword into its chest. Then he held up his orb and started to say the spell that would forever capture the worst monster

Jolie had ever faced. The beast wailed as the spell went on, Ledger's voice a powerful trance that reined the monster in.

When Ledger finished it, he came over and knelt next to her. He put his hand on her cheek and asked, "Are you okay?"

She nodded, still a little shaken, and her throat felt raw from the constriction. "Just a little dizzy," she managed to garble out. "It was the same Screamer that took your mom. I'm so sorry, Ledger. I didn't know."

His eyes got hard as he stared at the orb that contained a murderer. "I heard it tell you that. I knew I'd never be able to live with myself if I didn't kill it."

She reached up and put her hand over his. "I'm glad you did."

He pressed his lips together, his expression conflicted. "I'm sorry you didn't get to do it. You've been hunting it for years, waiting for the chance to get your revenge."

She shook her head. "I don't care who killed it; I'm just glad it's gone and no one else's parents will become one of its victims."

"It's gone as long as it doesn't heal from those wounds, and no one ever breaks this orb," he said.

"No one will *ever* break that orb. I'll put it in a special spot and ward the crap out of it."

Ledger's lips slid up into a charming smile and Jolie wondered what he could possibly be happy about. "We beat them."

"We did," she agreed. "Thanks to your help. I couldn't have done it alone."

"So," he said, leaning down over her. "I'm done waiting."

His lips met hers in a searing kiss, soft and rough at the same time. She threaded her hands through his hair, pulling him closer. And as she kissed him, her very first kiss, she had the realization that she no longer wanted to be alone. She wanted this man, this incredible man, in her life for the rest of time. Her heart was bursting as she came to the only conclusion possible: she loved Ledger Cross, and she always would. For Ledger, and only Ledger, she could take the armor off, and that knowledge meant everything in the world.

He pulled back and looked at her, brushing hair from her cheek. She didn't cringe at his gaze. "We all have scars, Jolie. Some are more visible than others. But they all make us who we are. And they're beautiful." He held her eyes. "*You* are beautiful." He leaned down and lightly brushed her lips. "Your scars," he said, moving past her mouth to the marks on her right cheek and then down her neck, kissing each one, "are beautiful."

He spent several minutes kissing years of pain away that had been trapped in the marks, and when he was finished he said, "I love you, Jolie."

A tear escaped her eye. He kissed it away. "I love your fire, your strength, and how much you care about others. I love that you spend your life fighting things that people don't even know exist just to keep them safe and you do it all self-lessly. I love every part of you Jolie —inside and out."

Ledger kissed her again.

And Jolie's first kiss, and all their kisses after, were perfect.

The End

ABOUT THE AUTHOR

Angela Corbett graduated from Westminster College and previously worked as a journalist, freelance writer, and director of communications and marketing. She lives in Utah with her extremely supportive husband, and loves classic cars, traveling, and chasing their five-pound Pomeranian, Pippin—who is just as mischievous as his hobbit namesake. She's the author of Young Adult, New Adult, and Adult fiction—with lots of kissing. She writes under two names, Angela Corbett, and Destiny Ford.

http://www.angelacorbett.com/

Join my newsletter to get a free book!
http://eepurl.com/KhLAn

facebook.com/AuthorAngelaCorbett

twitter.com/angcorbett

instagram.com/byangcorbett